Why Me?

Nate's Journal

Why Me?

by K.E. Calder

Vanwell Publishing Limited
St. Catharines, Ontario

Vanwell Publishing acknowledges the financial support of the
Government of Canada through the Book Publishing Industry
Development Program for our publishing activities.

Vanwell Publishing acknowledges the Government of Ontario through
the Ontario Media Development Corporation's Book Initiative.

Vanwell Publishing Limited
P.O. Box 2131
1 Northrup Crescent
St. Catharines, ON
Canada L2R 7S2
sales@vanwell.com
1-800-661-6136

Produced and designed by Tea Leaf Press Inc.
www.tealeafpress.com

Printed in Canada

National Library of Canada Cataloguing in Publication

Calder, Kate, 1974–
    Why me? / K.E. Calder.

(Nate's journal)
ISBN 1-55068-129-X

    I. Title. II. Series: Calder, Kate, 1974- . Nate's journal.

PS8555.A46515W49 2004   jC813'.6   C2004-901166-9

For Jeff

Journal of Nate Brown

STOP!!!!

DO NOT READ
THIS BOOK

OR ELSE!!!!

November 1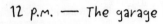

12 p.m. — The garage

I need a cell phone.

Grade eight is turning out to be not so bad. But it would be even better if I had a cell phone.

Frankie got one for his birthday. He showed it to me and Trevor this morning. We were shooting hoops at the basketball court.

"Hey guys, check this out," Frankie said. He pulled the cell phone out of his pocket. He turned it on, and it beeped a little song.

Trevor said, "Is that yours?"

Frankie laughed. "Yeah!" he said.

I said, "How did YOU get a cell phone?"

Frankie said, "It was a birthday present. My parents gave it to me this morning. They woke up early, and my mom made me a huge breakfast."

I said, "It's your birthday? Why didn't you tell us it was your birthday?"

He said, "What's there to tell? It's my birthday. I'm telling you now."

Trevor said, "I can't believe you have your own cell phone."

Frankie said, "Yeah, I know! Monty doesn't even have one. He can't believe that I have one. Ha." Monty is Frankie's older brother. He's in high school and has his own truck.

Trevor said all he got for his birthday were clothes. That sucks. Frankie said when you turn thirteen it's a big deal. Your parents owe you a big present.

I told them my thirteenth birthday is coming up. It's in a few weeks. Frankie said I should start hinting now for what I want. He said that's what he did. And he ended up with a cell phone. I wonder what my mom and dad have planned. Frankie's right. I should start dropping hints. A cell phone would be great. But my parents aren't as cool as Frankie's. I have a feeling no one's parents are that cool.

Frankie said he had to go. He had a lot of people to call. He said he's having a party tonight. We're the first people to know about it.

Frankie left, and Trevor and I shot some more hoops. Trevor is on the school basketball team. I tried out, too. But I'm not really the basketball type. All the guys who made the team went to basketball camp. I didn't really have a chance.

After a while we went back to Trevor's house. Trevor's mom was at the top of the stairs. She was in a housecoat, and her hair was messy. She had black stuff under her eyes. I think she just woke up.

She said, "Where were you two? It's Saturday."

Trevor said, "Shooting hoops."

She said, "But it's so early."

Trevor said, "It's eleven o'clock."

Trevor's mom rubbed her eyes and yawned.

She said, "Trevor, can you put on a pot of coffee, please?"

Trevor and I went into the kitchen. He turned on the coffeemaker. He scooped dry coffee into the top. He poured in water. Then he took two cups from the cupboard.

I said, "You drink coffee, too?"

Trevor said, "Yeah, don't you?"

I have never had coffee. I don't think my parents would even let me have it. I've had coffee cake, though. And I didn't really like it. So I just said, "No, I never touch the stuff."

"Whatever," said Trevor. He put three spoonfuls of sugar into his cup. Next he poured in some chocolate milk.

4 p.m. — My bedroom

So now here I am in my room. I'm going over to Frankie's house at seven o'clock. He called every kid in grade eight at Emery Public. He even called some of the ones in grade seven. His basement is going to be packed.

Miranda de Silva will be there. She just started at Emery at the beginning of this year. She's the best-looking girl in our class. I think she is the best-looking girl in the whole school. And the coolest. She has all sorts of skater T-shirts. I've talked to her a few times. Well, we sit beside each other in music class.

I play the flute. I didn't choose the flute, of course. On the first day of school it was the only instrument left. I'm the only guy in the class who plays the flute. That sucks. At least I get to sit with Miranda. So I guess it has its good points.

Miranda almost had to move to another school. Mrs. Berger and her parents wanted to put her in a gifted school. She's really smart. But she begged her parents to stay at Emery. I didn't think anyone would beg to stay at Emery. But it would be hard to leave in the middle of the school year. She had to make new friends in September. Doing it all over again would be really hard.

6:55 p.m. — My room

My sister, Tammy, just walked into my room. Without knocking, I might add. She's in grade six. But she acts like she's in high school or something. She's wearing a dumb top that shows her belly button. Mom will never let her out of the house like that. I don't even know why she tries. Tammy says that Mom says I have to walk her over to the

Schmits' house. She's babysitting there tonight. It's a long way from Frankie's house. I'm going to be late for the party. She smiled at me and then left my room. I'm freaking out now. Why can't my parents just drive her? Why can't the Schmits just come and pick her up? I told my mom that it would make me late for Frankie's party. She just said that the party could wait. That's how much she knows. The party will start and go on without me. I could be missing major social events. Crap.

Have to go. Tammy just yelled my name from downstairs. Her royal highness is ready. I should get a walking fee. Five percent of the night's babysitting earnings would be fair, I think.

November 2

11:45 a.m. — The kitchen

I was right. By the time I got to the party I was late. A full twenty minutes late. I walked up to the house. Frankie's brother Monty was just pulling out of the driveway in his truck.

He yelled, "Hey! Have fun with the rest of the kiddies." He backed out onto the road and took off. I walked in the front door and through the house. I could hear music coming from the basement. I went downstairs. It was really dark. Except everything white was glowing. What the heck? I looked down at myself. A thousand tiny pieces of lint were glowing on my black T-shirt.

Lint

A lot of people were sitting around on sofas. There was a rolled-up rug along one wall. Some kids were sitting on that, too.

"Hey Nate," I heard a voice say. I looked over toward the space under the stairs. It was Frankie. He smiled and his teeth glowed in the dark. He stepped out of the darkness. I realized Suki was standing under the stairs with him. They were standing really close together and holding hands with just their fingers. He left her for a minute. He came over to where I was standing in the middle of the room.

"What are you doing?" I asked.

He said, "Nothing."

"Why are your teeth so white?" I asked.

Frankie smiled again. His white teeth gave me the creeps. "I put a black light in here. It makes light colors glow in the dark. Cool, huh?"

I couldn't take my eyes off Frankie's freaky white teeth. "Uh huh."

I said, "So, did your parents go out?"

He said, "No, I'm not that lucky. They're in their bedroom watching a movie. But they said they would leave us alone to party all night."

I said, "Cool." If it were my party, my parents would be down here. They'd be making us all pin the tail on the donkey or something. Frankie is lucky he's the youngest. His parents were used to their kids getting older. They didn't treat Frankie like a little kid. I mean, he got a cell phone. That's pretty cool.

I spotted Trevor, Jason, and Ramesh by the sliding glass doors. They were sitting on lawn chairs. I decided I would look around for Miranda

in a minute. Ramesh waved and shouted, "Hey, Nate. Over here."

I was just about to walk over there when I heard a girl say my name. I turned around expecting to see Miranda. It was Ashley.

"Hi, Nate," she said.

I said, "Oh. Hi, Ashley. Why aren't you hanging out with Suki?"

"Because she's talking to Frankie. So are you having a good time?" she said.

I said, "Yeah, I guess."

She said, "This is going to be a good party." She folded her arms and smiled so big her mouth shone a neon white.

I said, "Yeah, whatever."

"You want to talk?" she asked.

"Actually, I'm just going to talk to the guys right now," I said. What did she want to talk to me about anyway?

"Okay. Hey, when we play Spin the Bottle you should sit across from me."

Was she kidding? I just grunted and walked away as fast as I could. Spin the Bottle. As if we were going to play that. We played that game at parties in grade six. Grade seven, maybe. I have only ever really played it once. I kissed Cheri LeBlanc. Actually I kissed her chin. But hey, I was in grade six. I had bad aim.

After a while, Frankie came over to me and the guys. He said that he wanted to play Spin the Bottle. Figures. He just wanted a chance to kiss Suki.

Everyone went to the middle of the room. We all sat in a big circle. Frankie got an old bottle from his parents' wine cellar. He put it in the middle of the circle. I looked around to see where everyone was. Ashley was sitting straight across from me. Right beside her was Miranda. And Miranda was almost right across from me! I hadn't seen her come in. The chances of me getting to kiss her were...well they were like one in twenty.
But still, it *could* happen.

"Birthday guy first," someone yelled over the music. Frankie reached for the bottle. He gave it a good spin. We all watched as it spun around and around. Finally it started to slow down. Slower, slower.

Finally it stopped. Everyone looked at who it was pointing to. Ashley. She laughed and looked at the floor. Then they both crawled across the circle. Just as they were about to kiss, Frankie's cell phone rang. He reached down and flipped it open.

"Hello?" he said. He didn't say anything for a minute. Then he said, "No, Mom, we're fine. No, we don't need more drinks. Okay. Okay. Good-bye." He shut the phone and put it back in his pocket. Then he leaned forward and kissed Ashley really quickly. I don't think their lips touched. It looked like a fake beside-the-mouth kiss to me. But whatever.

Next it was Ashley's turn to spin the bottle. I felt a shiver of fear as the bottle slowed down. It slowed down in front of me. But it kept going and came to a stop at Ramesh. They crawled across the circle and kissed quickly.

This went on for several more turns. At one point Trevor's spin landed on Frankie. Everyone laughed. Frankie said that Trevor was allowed to spin again. He got Miranda. I couldn't believe he was going to get to kiss Miranda. I watched them crawl across the circle to each other. Their kiss seemed to take place in slow motion. I wanted to look away, but I couldn't take my eyes off them. I hope she doesn't fall in love with Trevor because of this.

Then it was Miranda's turn. She spun the bottle. It landed on Stu Leatherland. I kind of wished it had been me. Stu spun the bottle next. It landed on Daria Williams. She was sitting right beside me. She spun next, and when it stopped it was pointing right at me. So much for sitting across from the person you wanted to kiss. At least I didn't have to crawl across the circle.

We leaned toward each other. I kept my eyes open and tried to look at her mouth. Not the chin, not the chin, not the chin. My lips touched hers. We kissed for a split second and then pulled away. I sat back in my spot. By that time, almost everyone had been kissed. The game was over. Thank God. Spin the Bottle is for kids.

kiss

don't kiss

November 3

The bus — Back seat

Our whole music class is on a field trip today. We went into the city to see the symphony. Miss Mirel said that we would hear what we are supposed to sound like. I have a pretty good feeling that we'll never sound like that.

The symphony is really boring. There's nothing to see. You just sit there. And listen. I think they should put a huge TV screen over the instruments. They could show a music video. It would be a symphony music video. They could still make a really cool video. I couldn't even look around at all the kids from different schools. It was too dark. I sat with the guys. Finally. Usually I have to sit with all the flute girls. I miss out on all of Trevor and Jason's jokes.

We tried joking around at the symphony. But Miss Mirel came and sat right in front of us. I looked back at all the faces of kids sitting behind me. Miranda waved when she saw me looking!

We're almost back at the school now. Thank God. One of our horn players puked. He said he was going to puke. But the bus couldn't pull over in time to let him out. So he just stood in middle of the bus and puked. That made some kids around him almost puke. I would have for sure if I were sitting beside him. I can smell it from here. It's nasty. All the windows are open. And it's pretty cold outside.

I think if I was going to puke, I would do it behind a seat. Not in the middle of the bus. Or better yet, out the window. That would be gross for people in the cars behind the bus. Imagine if puke sprayed out of a bus and onto your car.

8 p.m. — My bedroom

It was my turn to help my mom clean up after dinner. My dad was also in the kitchen. I figured this would be the perfect time to drop some hints about my birthday.

I said, "Frankie had a really cool birthday party in his basement."

hint
  hint

21

My dad said, "Oh yeah?"

I said, "Yeah, and his parents gave him the coolest gift. Guess what it was."

My dad said, "What?"

I said, "A cell phone."

My mom laughed and said, "What does Frankie need with a cell phone? He's only thirteen."

I said, "Yeah, I know. It's really cool and it has call display."

My dad said, "What is the world coming to?"

This wasn't really going the way I had planned. I said, "His parents can call him anytime and know where he is." I thought that might sell them on the idea. You can trick parents into doing something if they think it will be good for them.

My mom said, "You don't need one of those. You tell us where you're going in the first place."

"What if I want to go someplace after school? I could call and let you know," I said.

My Dad said, "We'll give you a quarter. You can call from a pay phone."

I said, "A pay phone? Yeah, right." My parents just looked at each other. It's hard to tell what it means when they do that. Maybe they're going to get me a cell phone for my birthday. And they're just trying to throw me off track.

November 4 ᐱᐱᐱ

6 p.m. — My bedroom

When I got home from school today there was a sign on the front lawn. A "For Sale" sign. Just then, Tammy rode up on her bike. She stopped and got off. We both walked up the driveway toward the sign. Then we just stopped and looked at it for a minute. How could our house be for sale?

I said, "Was this here this morning?"

Tammy shook her head. "Uh uh."

We went inside. My mom was in the kitchen at the sink.

I said, "What's going on?"

Tammy said, "Yeah, why is there a 'For Sale' sign on our lawn?"

My mom said, "We have put the house up for sale."

"NO!" I said. It was the only thing that I could spit out of my mouth.

"Yeah, no way!" said Tammy.

"What? Why? When?" I said loudly.

"Don't panic. We're not moving out of town. We want to move into something a bit bigger."

"Why do we need bigger?" I said.

My mom said, "Your father is going to be working from home more. We need a house with a home office."

"I like this house," I said. "It's fine. Why can't dad work in the spare bedroom? You could make that into an office."

"Yeah, I don't want to leave this house. No way," said Tammy.

My mom said, "Look, we have wanted to buy a bigger house for a while now. You'll both have bigger rooms. Maybe your own TV room in the basement. You'll like it. You'll see. And we just put it up for sale today. It could take months to sell. You don't have to pack up your stuff just yet."

I can't believe this house is for sale. This is the only house I've ever lived in. But I guess if we're not moving out of town, it won't be that bad. I'll still be here with all my friends. It would be kind of cool to have a bigger room. It's pretty crowded in here. Maybe I can have a party like Frankie's in the new basement.

November 6 ≈

My locker

I just got out of math class. Mr. Sweet handed back our math tests today. I got a "D"! A "D"! I've never got a "D" before. On the last test I got a "C." I'm getting worse. At this rate I could fail. I can't believe it. I hate math.

Mr. Sweet told me to wait after class. So I did. He said he was surprised that I got a "D." I said, so was I. He told me that he is going to give the class a small test tomorrow. He said this is my chance to make up my grade.

He looked right at me and said, "Study."

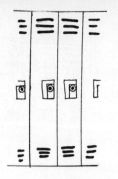

When I got to my locker, Suki was here. The door was open, and she was brushing her hair. I thought that maybe I had the wrong locker. But no, it was my locker. The one I share with Frankie. I asked her what she was doing.

She said, "Brushing my hair."

I asked her where Frankie was. She said she didn't know.

I said, "How did you open the locker?"

She said, "Frankie told me how to open it." She must have seen the look of anger on my face. So she said, "He said I could open it to use the mirror to brush my hair."

I said, "Why don't you get your own mirror?"

She said, "What's the big deal, Nate? Jeesh." She closed the door and locked it. Then she flipped her long black hair over her shoulder and walked away. Hello? I was just about to go in the locker. But never mind. I'll just open the lock again.

I can't believe Frankie. I know he likes Suki, but come on! I don't want any girls opening *my* locker to brush *their* hair. Aren't there mirrors in the

26

girls' bathrooms? Why do they have to brush their hair in the hall? Why do they have to brush their hair at all?

8 p.m. — My bedroom

I cannot afford to fail math. If I have to stay here next year with the grade sevens…well, let's not even go there.

I have a plan. It isn't the best plan. In fact, it could get me into trouble. But I've got to ace this test. I'm writing some math equations on a tiny sheet of paper. The paper is really small. I'm writing really tiny. I'm going to wear my soccer sweater tomorrow. It has really long arms. I'll be able to keep the paper inside the sweater. Then I can slide it into my hand when the teacher isn't looking.

It's not really cheating. At least I don't think it is. It's not like I have the answers. I just can't remember the equations. And I need to know them to answer the problems. It's impossible. I've written half of them out already. There are only a few more to do. It's taken me a lot longer than I thought. I had to start over a couple of times. My writing was too big.

November 7 ✍

My locker

I just took Mr. Sweet's math test. I was so nervous that I was sweating. I wanted to look at the paper in my sweater. But I couldn't. I thought for sure I would get caught.

Mr. Sweet handed out the test. I did the first question no problem. Then I did the second. And the third. I didn't even need the little sheet of paper! I was remembering the stuff I had written. It was a good thing, too. I think Mr. Sweet was looking at me the whole time.

I'm going to write everything down on a tiny sheet of paper next time, too. But I don't think I'll actually bring it to the test next time.

Now here I am at my locker. I can't open my stupid lock. What is wrong with it? Why can't I open my own locker? I've tried it at least twenty-five times. It won't work.

7:45 p.m. — My bedroom

After school I still couldn't open my lock. Finally Frankie showed up. He opened the lock easily.

I said, "How the heck did you do that?"

He said, "It's a new lock."

I said, "What! You can't just change the lock and not tell me. How was I supposed to open it?"

He said that he was going to tell me this morning. But I got here before he did. So he figured he'd just wait until he saw me. That's just great. Except that I couldn't open our locker all day.

I said, "Why do we need a new lock anyway?" He said that he and Suki traded locks.

I said, "What! Why?" He said it was just for fun. They both know how to open each other's lockers, so they decided to trade. That's the dumbest thing I've ever heard. I told him to make sure he let me know if he was going to change locks on me.

November 8 ◡̈

Noon — The garage

My parents are going nuts. They are on some wild cleaning kick. I had to get out of the house. They were driving me nuts, too. There is some sort of "open house" going on here today. It means the place has to be cleaner than humanly possible. Then a whole bunch of strangers march through our place. I asked my mom, "What if they go through our stuff?" She says no one will go through our stuff. I asked her how she knew that. She said that there will be real estate agents here. They will be keeping an eye on people.

We all have to leave for three hours for people to snoop through. My parents asked if we wanted to go to the mall with them. I said I'd rather go to Ramesh's to skate. I'm just eating my lunch first. My mom said I had to eat out here in the garage. I'd leave crumbs in the kitchen.

I hope no one goes through my stuff.

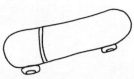

November 10

Mr. Sweet handed back our math tests today. He walked around and laid them face down on our desks. Trevor picked up his. He made a fart noise with his mouth and then turned it over again. Then Mr. Sweet came around to my desk. He stopped beside me and looked down at me. He said, "Nate," and raised his eyebrows. Then he laid the test down on my desk.

What did that mean? What did raised eyebrows mean? I had done badly again? I lifted up the paper a bit. I peeked at the mark. It was an "A-." An "A-"! I flipped over the test. There were check marks all over the place. I looked around. Some of the girls were showing each other their marks. Most kids were putting their tests in their binders. I wanted to show everyone the test and shout, "Hey, I got an 'A-'!" But I didn't. I just put my test in my binder quietly.

Trevor said, "Brown, why are you smiling?"

I said, "No reason," and wiped the smile off my face. I didn't want to look like I cared or anything.

He looked at my test and saw the "A-." He just made another fart sound with his mouth and looked away.

6 p.m. — My bedroom

I showed my parents my math test at dinner. They were really happy.

My mom said, "See? Studying really pays off." I didn't tell her that I didn't really study. That I made a cheat sheet but didn't use it at the last minute.

I decided to hint about the cell phone again.

I said, "I wanted to call you with the good news as soon as I found out."

My mom said, "Really, Nate? That's sweet."

I said, "Yeah, I could have if I had a cell phone. I wouldn't have had to wait until I got home."

My dad laughed a bit. He said, "Yes, that's really thoughtful of you, Nate. Always thinking of your parents."

I said, "I am. That's why I need a cell phone. For you guys."

My dad put another forkful of salad in his mouth. He grunted something. I looked at my mom. She made a face that said, "Yeah, right."

November 11 ☺

Noon — The lunch room

I told my mom this morning that I could use a new DVD player. I don't know if they have my birthday present yet. But it would be cool to watch movies in my own room. I would never have to watch Tammy's stupid TV shows. My mom was packing a lunch. She stopped and looked at me for a couple of seconds.

"Nate, you don't have a DVD player. How could you need a *new* one?"

"I mean I could use one in general," I said.

She said, "What are you going to do with a DVD player? You don't even have a TV."

"Well, I'd need the TV too, of course," I said.

"Oh, of course," said my mom. "Of course." I don't think she was for real, though.

After lunch, this grade seven kid walked up to my locker. I've seen him around, but I've never talked to him.

He walked right up to me and said, "Hey." At first I didn't even think he was talking to me. I looked behind me, but there was no one there. I just looked at him. He said, "Cool skate mags." I had no idea what he was talking about.

"What?" I said.

He said, "Your skateboarding mags. They're cool." There were no skate mags in my locker. What was with this kid?

I looked at him and said, "Where?"

He said, "In your room."

Again, I said, "What?!"

He said, "I was in your room. My parents were looking at your house this weekend. I saw your room. Cool skating mags." I couldn't believe it. This little snot had been in my room. Who else had been in my room this weekend? I looked around. A couple of people looked at me. Were they in my

34

room, too? My room is not a public park. Everyone can't just walk through and look at my stuff!

"You better not have gone through my stuff!" I said loudly.

"I didn't," he said.

"You better not!" I said.

"I didn't!" he said. "I just looked at your magazines."

I yelled, "I don't care."

The kid took a couple of steps back. Then he turned around and walked away quickly.

I've just checked my room. Nothing is missing. That kid is so lucky.

November 12

11:30 p.m. — My bedroom

It's almost midnight. In half an hour I will be thirteen. I can't wait for tomorrow. I wonder what my parents have planned. I can't wait to be thirteen. Twelve is so little kid. I can't believe I'm still twelve even right now. I feel like I'm already thirteen.

thirteen thirteen

I even feel kind of fourteen. In olden days, boys went through a lot when they turned thirteen. They went hunting and became men and stuff.

November 13

7:30 a.m. — My bedroom

It's my birthday. I've been awake for an hour now. I thought my parents would come into my room to give me my present. That's what Frankie's parents did. But my parents have never really done that. They usually say "happy birthday" when I go down for breakfast. So I guess I'll wait for breakfast.

8:50 a.m. — Boys' bathroom

Okay, nothing at breakfast. I didn't get a "happy birthday" or even a card. That's weird. Usually my mom makes me pancakes on my birthday. Maybe I'm too old for that now. Frankie says parents consider turning thirteen a big deal. They must be saving my birthday stuff until the end of day. That's

when adults sing "Happy Birthday" to each other. At the end of the day. That's fine. I'll just wait until I get home.

12:05 p.m. — The lunch room

I think I know what is going on. My parents are throwing me a surprise party. No one has said "happy birthday" all day. Not my parents, not my friends, or my teachers. Not even my little sister. There can only be one reason. They are pretending to forget. That way they can surprise me later on. Okay, I'm game. I'll play along. This will be fun.

5:32 p.m. — The living room

They are really dragging this out. They are all pretending that it's not my birthday. My sister is talking on the phone. My mom is checking her e-mail and my dad just sat down to watch the news. How are they going to get all my friends in here without me seeing? Maybe I should hang out in my room for a while to make it easier for them.

I came up to my bedroom. I didn't hear anything going on downstairs. No doorbell or loud voices. But they'll be quiet because it's my surprise party. My mom called me down to dinner. I thought, "This is it." I went downstairs ready to be surprised in the hall.

Nothing.

I took a deep breath and peeked around the corner to the kitchen. Nothing. Just my family sitting at the table. My dad was scooping stew onto plates. Stew? They know I don't like stew. Is this part of the plan to throw me off track?

He said, "Nate, what are you doing? Let's hurry up and eat. Your mom and I have an important meeting tonight." Aha! An important meeting. Could that be about my birthday? I think so. I played along and sat down at the table. After dinner there was no dessert. A sure sign that birthday cake is on its way.

Now I'm upstairs. Waiting.

8:00 p.m. — The stairs

They really did have a meeting. There are some people here. Two women and a man. They have been here for an hour. My parents are in the dining room with them.

I'm starting to think there's no surprise party. But that's okay. I'm sure my parents just need to take care of this meeting. Then we'll have the cake, and they'll give me my present.

8:30 p.m. — My bedroom. Again.

The people have gone, but still nothing has happened. I went downstairs to see what they were up to. They were just watching TV. This is getting really weird. Do they just expect me to wait forever?

10:00 p.m. — The bathroom

My parents have just gone to bed. I can't figure out what is going on. Did they forget my birthday? Impossible. Are they planning a super surprise?

?

?

 It would be really cool to have a cake and get a present at the stroke of midnight. They must be pretending to go to sleep so they can surprise me.

10:45 p.m. — My bedroom

Now I am pretending to go to sleep. I'm sure that's what they are waiting for.

12:01 a.m. — My bedroom

They forgot.

November 14

3:30 p.m. — The garage

Today was really weird. I feel like my birthday never happened. I was going to say something at breakfast. But then I thought that maybe I had the date wrong. Maybe *today* was really November 13. Not yesterday.

When I got to first class I looked at the board. It said November 14. I was right. Yesterday was my birthday.

I should have said something at breakfast. My family would feel really bad. And it serves them right. Thirteen is a big deal and they blew it. This is the worst thing that has ever happened to me. If your parents don't make a big deal about your birthday, who will? No one. No one cares about me. I may as well stay out here in the garage all night. Maybe they'll think I've run away and call the police. Then when the police come, they'll look all over the place. It will be on the eleven o'clock news. Boy, thirteen, runs away. Cut to my parents crying and begging for me to come back. "We're so sorry we forgot your birthday, Nate. Please come back!"

7:00 p.m. — My bedroom

My mom called me in for dinner from the garage. And nothing. Still no "happy birthday" or birthday cake. I decided to say nothing. I'm waiting them out now. I want to see just how long it will take for

them to remember. I hardly said anything at dinner.
I just kept staring at the food on my plate.

I came up to my room to play computer games. A while later, I heard a knock on the door.

I said, "Come in." The door opened. Both my mom and dad were standing in the doorway. Right  away I knew something was up. They never come to talk to me at the same time. My father was standing behind my mom. His hands were on her shoulders. My mom was holding her hands together. Neither of them said anything at first. I just sat there.

Then my mom said, "Oh, Nate!" And I knew they had remembered. She held out her hands and stepped toward me. She leaned down and hugged me while I was sitting at my computer. "We're so sorry. Happy birthday. Happy late birthday."

"Why didn't you say anything, Nate?" my dad asked. I just sat there. I felt stupid saying that I thought it was all a big plan to surprise me. And I felt mean for wanting them to feel bad.

"Well, we're going to make it up to you. Starting right now," my mom said. She turned her head toward the hall, "Tammy, you can come in now." Tammy walked in the room slowly. Her head was down.

She held out her hand and handed me a card.

She said, "Happy birthday, Nate." She had made the card out of light blue paper. On the front was a picture of a half-pipe. She had cut it out of a magazine. I opened it. It read, "It sucks that everyone forgot your birthday." She had drawn a dog with huge ears standing on a skateboard. There was a tear falling from one of its big sad eyes.

I said, "Thanks, Tammy."

Then my dad went to the hallway and brought in a big present.

He said, "We picked these out for you a while ago. Hope you like them." I ripped off the wrapping paper and opened the box. There was a new set of cool pads, a new shirt, and new wheels. They are the ones I've been wanting since the summer. And I didn't even hint about those on purpose.

I said, "This is great. Thanks, Mom and Dad."

My mom said, "We have one more present. We want to take you and your friends to the skatepark downtown tomorrow afternoon. You can invite as many friends as you'd like."

"Thanks!" I said. This wasn't turning out to be a bad birthday after all.

My dad said, "You were really nice even though we forgot. You have also done a good job keeping your room clean. And you got a good mark on your math test. I think thirteen is a big year for you, Nate."

I said, "Yeah, I guess."

My mom looked at my dad. Then she said, "I guess we should explain why we forgot your birthday. Yesterday there were some people here, as you both know. They were here to see the house."

"Did they like it?" asked Tammy.

"Yes they did. In fact, they made us an offer. And we accepted. We are going to sell it to them," she said.

I said, "But—but I thought it could take months to sell."

My dad said, "It can. But this time it happened quickly. We were lucky."

"Lucky? But now we have to move," I said. "Where are we going to go?"

My dad said, "We're thinking of buying a house on Rideout Road."

"Rideout Road? Where's that? I thought you said we wouldn't have to move out of town."

My mom said, "We aren't. It's across town. It's a bigger house. I think you will both really like it."

"Well then, can I have a new desk?" said Tammy.

"Yes, a new desk would be a good idea," said my dad.

"And a lava lamp?" Tammy said.

"Don't push your luck," said Mom.

The new people are moving into this house in January. We're going to have to pack up by the end of the year. And I just did a major cleanup of my room. What a waste of time. Now I'm going to have to go through all my stuff all over again.

I'm going to miss this room. But Dad said the new house has a pool. A bigger room and a pool. Cool, I guess.

I like my skateboarding stuff. It's not a cell phone, but I think it's pretty cool, anyway. Frankie was right. Thirteen is a big deal.

November 15 ᴧᴧᴧᴧ

7 p.m.

Today my parents and I picked up Trevor and Jason and Ramesh. We drove downtown to the skatepark. My parents dropped us off. They went and did something else for the afternoon. It's like they finally get it.

It was pretty cold, but there were a ton of other kids there. We had to take turns taking runs and doing tricks. A couple of times I almost ran into people. Trevor actually did run into another skater. It knocked the wind out of him. He had to sit down for a while.

That cool skater kid I met the last time was there. I didn't know it was him at first. His hat was pulled down over his ears. I wished I had my hat. My ears were really cold. He had some friends with him this time. They were all just as good as he was. I asked him about the competitions he goes in. We gave each other our e-mail addresses. His name is Martin Cruz. He is going to e-mail me about skateboarding stuff. Cool.

I was standing at the top of the bowl waiting for a free space. A girl on the other side dropped down and then came up right beside me. She flipped up her board. She had a pink and orange hat with a big pom-pom. It had strings that hung down to her shoulders. Her turtleneck was pulled up  over her chin. There were hardly ever girls at the skatepark. And never any who could skate like that.

I looked down. All the kids were up at the sides. It was my turn to go. I swallowed. I looked ahead and dropped down into the bowl. For a second I hoped I wouldn't fall in front of a girl. But before I knew it I was up on the other side. I couldn't remember skating down. All I could think of was a pink and orange hat with a big pom-pom.

November 17 🌿

Lunchtime — Boys' bathroom

I can't believe this. I'm going to have to go to a different school.

I found out in music class. Miss Mirel got called to the office. She told us to keep practicing our music scales. Yeah right. I turned around to tell Trevor and Jason that I'm going to have a pool. I knew they would think that was really cool. We could plan a pool party in the summer. Trevor asked where the new house was.

I said, "Rideout Road."

Trevor said, "That's on the other side of town."

I said, "Yeah, so?"

Trevor looked at me. "So, you'll be out of this school area. You'll have to go to Bunting Public."

I said, "What? No way. I've gone to school here my whole life. They'll let me keep coming here."

48

Bunting Public bites!

Jason said, "I don't think so. How are you going to get here? Emery school buses don't go to the other side of town."

I said, "My mom will drive me."

Jason said, "It doesn't matter. They won't let you. You have to change schools." I was sure they would let me keep coming here. What did Jason know, anyway?

"It's true, Nate." Miranda turned around in her chair. "That's why I had to come here. I went to Bunting Public. My street was the next one over from Rideout. Then my parents moved to this side of town. I had to start coming here."

I said, "Oh."

Trevor said, "See?" Miss Mirel came back in the classroom.

I said, "Shut up," and turned back around. I felt like I had been kicked in the gut. What was I going to do? I hated this school and couldn't wait to go to high school. But I didn't want to leave before the year was over. I didn't want to finish grade eight at another crappy public school. With no friends. And I wouldn't be able to go to Hilldale High either. I'd have to go to Eastlea High. Everyone in town calls it Greasy Eastlea. I don't want to be a greaser from Greasy Eastlea. No way.

Miss Mirel tapped her pointer stick. Everyone raised their instruments. I raised mine too, but I couldn't blow into it. The class started playing. I just moved my fingers and pretended. How could my parents do this to me?

I don't care what I have to do. I am not leaving without a fight. I'm not going to change schools just because I'm moving across town. I'm not going to let my parents push me around. Or any other adults for that matter. I looked up and Miss Mirel was looking at me. She didn't look happy. I mouthed, "Sorry" and started playing my flute for real.

2 p.m. — Math class

I have to think of a way to stay at this school. What can I do? Maybe my mom or dad could drive me across town every morning. I would never tell the school that I had moved. They would never know.

 help me!

I'd have to talk my parents into it, though. My mom would never agree to it. First of all, she would have to lie. She hates lying. She almost never does it. Besides, I want to figure this out on my own. I'm thirteen. I don't need my parents to take care of all my problems.

I could ask one of my friends if I could live with them. Maybe Frankie. His parents seem cool. Not Trevor. I don't think his mom likes me very much. My parents would freak out if I said I was moving in with a friend. Well, too bad. If they can move, then so can I.

4 p.m. — My bedroom

I can't believe my mother. First she decides to move across town and mess up my life. Then she interrupts the most important phone calls I've ever had.

I had just got home from school when the phone rang. I was on my computer. The phone was right beside me, so I answered it.

A voice said, "Hello, is Nate there?" Only it wasn't one of my friends' voices. It was a girl.

I thought, "Great. Frankie gave Ashley my phone number." So I said, "Yeah, this is Nate. What's it to you?"

The voice said, "Oh. Hi, Nate. It's Miranda."

I sat up. I cleared my throat. I held onto the phone tightly. I said, "Hi! I mean, hi, how are you?"

Miranda said, "Fine, how are you?"

"Fine. How are you?" I said.

"Fine." Nothing. Why was she calling me? Just to talk? What was I going to talk about? I wasn't prepared for this. She should have warned me in music that she was going to call.

"I guess you're wondering why I'm calling," she said.

"No. Well, yes," I said.

She said, "I thought of something after music class. Something about you moving schools. I thought I should tell you about it." Was she going to give me advice about Bunting? Was she going to offer pointers on making new friends?

I said, "What?"

She said, "I know someone who moved across town but stayed at the same school."

I said, "Really?" I couldn't believe it. "Who? What? How?"

She said, "Charlotte Williams. She was my neighbor across town. She was able to stay at Emery because of the music."

I said, "The music?"

"Yes. Last year her parents moved to the Bunting area. She's a great flute player. And Bunting doesn't have an after-school band. Also, the school board cut the after-school band at Eastlea. Charlotte wants to take flute in high school and then go to music college. She wants to be in the symphony someday. So they let her come back to Emery for the band. Now she goes to Hilldale High."

I said, "That's good. But what does that have to do with me?"

Miranda said, "Well, you play the flute."

I said, "Yeah, so?"

She said, "So you could say you need to come back for the music."

I said, "But I'm no good."

She said, "Yes, you are."

I said, "But I ha—" and then I stopped. Miranda didn't know how much I hated the flute. I had been pretending to like it all year. I don't know why. All I know is she liked flute, so I didn't want her to know that I hated it.

She said, "Well, you could just *say* that it was important to you. You could join the after-school band. Then they would have to let you come back."

"The after-school band?" I said. The thought of it made me want to puke. But if it meant getting to stay, I'd do it. Besides, it meant not having to go to Bunting. Or Greasy Eastlea.

"I'd hate for you to move," she said quietly.

"Really?" I said. I wasn't expecting this.

"Yeah. I mean, I like sitting beside you in music class. We have a lot of fun together." There was a noisy click. Right before she said, "We have a lot of fun together." Then Miranda stopped talking.

CLICK!

"Hello?" said a voice.

"Mom! I'm on the phone," I said. It's a good thing Miranda couldn't see me. I could feel my face go completely red.

"Oh, sorry." Then another click. It was just me and Miranda again.

"Okay," said Miranda. No one said anything for a minute. "Well, I just wanted to tell you that," she said quickly. "I have to go now." We said good-bye and hung up. I was happy that she had called. And I was even happier that I didn't have to change schools. Yes!

I picked up the phone again and called Frankie. I told him about having to change schools.

"So, I was thinking, can I move in with you?" I said.

"Yeah, right," said Frankie. Then he said, "My parents can't wait until I move out. They tell me all the time. I don't think they'll let me have a friend live in my room."

"Oh," I said. I told him about Miranda calling. Charlotte Williams. Joining the band. Having to play flute. Staying at Emery and then going to Hilldale next year. Miranda wanting me to stay.

Frankie 766-5441

Frankie said, "She said that? Cool. She will think you're staying to be near her. Chicks dig that." There was a click again. Just before he said, "Chicks dig that."

CLICK!

"Hello?" my mom's voice said loudly.

"*Mom!*"

"Oh, you're still on the phone. Sorry." She hung up. Can't I get a minute alone on the phone?

"You have to get a cell phone," said Frankie.

I said, "Yeah, tell me about it."

I guess that settles it. I'll join the band.

6 p.m. — The bus

I'm on the bus. I'm on my way to the library. I had to leave my house. When I say why, you will understand. I have to study for the next math test. But that's not why I had to leave my house. I was just going to study in my room but then my mom knocked on the door. I told her to come in. She

56

stepped inside and closed the door behind her. I watched quietly. She walked across my room and then sat on my bed. I twisted my chair around to face her. We both looked at each other for a minute.

I said, "What?"

At the same time, she said, "Nate."

I said, "What?" again.

She said, "Nate, I think we need to talk about something." I looked down and tried to think. What had I done in the last week? Ramesh and I had thrown a couple of balls up on the school roof. But no one knew about that. And that was hardly a big deal anyway. My room was pretty clean. I had been getting along with Tammy. Maybe she had found out about the prank from Halloween. Maybe the principal, Mrs. Berger, had phoned her. I'd be kicked out of Emery for good. Flute or no flute.

I looked up at my mom. She was leaning forward a bit. Her eyes were on me. She looked like she did last week when she and Dad forgot my birthday. Only that time she just looked sorry. This time she looked more weird than sorry.

I said, "About what?" with a straight face.

She said, "Well. We, um. We have never talked about girls." What? Girls? "You're going to be going out with girls. So, I think it's time we had a talk."

A talk? Gross! I just sat there. I didn't want to have a "talk." But I also wondered what she was going to say next. She cleared her throat.

"When girls and guys go out together, sometimes they—"

I didn't want to hear anymore. "Mom, I know."

She said, "Well, but sometimes they—"

"Mom! I know." I looked in the other direction. I could feel my face going red all over again. Was she really trying to have a sex talk with me?

She stopped trying to say whatever it was she was going to say. She said, "Nate, look at me. What do you know?"

"I know what girls and guys do," I said. I turned my head again and rolled my eyes.

"What do they do?"

"Mom! You know."

"Yes, I know. But I want to make sure you know," she said. She crossed her legs. She didn't seem unsure of herself anymore.

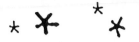

"I'm not saying," I said. As if I was going to tell my mom that stuff! We both knew, so fine. I mean I've known for years. Why did I have to say it? Whose mom makes them explain what they know?

"Listen, Nate, I heard you talking on the phone with a girl you like and—"

"I don't like her!" I said loudly. I couldn't believe she was saying this to me.

"Well, she likes you," said Mom.

"No she doesn't!" I said. Wait. "Why do you think that?" I asked.

"Because I heard her say you two have fun together," she said.

"Oh. That was nothing. I don't want to talk about this," I said. I really didn't.

"But I think we should get a few things straight," she said.

"No."

"Nate—"

"No!" Usually I would get in trouble for talking back. But she didn't say anything.

"Okay. I suppose this can wait," she said. She stood up.

"Good," I said.

She left the room. I pulled out my math book. But I couldn't focus. I was afraid she would try and get Dad to talk to me. So I packed up my stuff in my backpack. Now here I am on my way to the library.

November 18 ★

Today I was standing at my locker and I heard a click. I looked up just in time to be blinded by a huge flash. Ashley was standing in front of me with a camera.

I said, "What are you doing?"

She said, "Taking a picture of you."

I said, "Yeah, duh. Why?" I hoped she wasn't going to hang a picture of me in her locker. Or her room. She's so creepy.

"I'm taking pictures for the yearbook. Suki and I joined the yearbook club. I'm getting shots of kids around the halls."

I said, "Oh." That sounded normal to me.

She said, "That will be a great picture of you. I'll personally make sure it gets into the yearbook." And back to creepy again.

"Great," I said and reached for my math book.

Ashley said, "Hey, Nate, you should join the yearbook club, too. It's really fun. I'll show you how we choose the pictures and put the pages together."

I said, "Oh, uh, no thanks. I don't have time."

She said, "Why not?"

I said, "Because I've joined the band."

She just said, "Oh," in a sad voice. Then I shut my locker and said I had to go.

November 19 ⌒

Today after music class I stayed to talk to Miss Mirel. I wanted to ask her about joining the band. As the class was leaving, Miranda smiled at me. I told her during class that I was going to use her idea. I'm joining the band in order to stay at Emery.

Miss Mirel was really happy. She said she was pleased. She said it would take a lot of practice. Band practices are every Tuesday and Thursday after school. She said she is looking forward to having me in the band. The school has never had a boy flute player in the band. Yeah, no kidding!

She said I could sign out my flute for the night. I didn't really want to take my flute home. I did anyway. Just to show her that I'm into the band. She can't find out I'm faking it. I might not be allowed to stay at Emery.

Before I left the school I stopped by the office. I needed to talk to Mrs. Berger about joining the band. She was standing by the front desk when I walked in. Her big tall bun was balancing on top of her head as usual.

"Nate Brown, I haven't seen you in here in a while. What can I do for you?"

"I joined the band," I said quickly. "I joined the band and I play the flute."

She opened her eyes really wide. "That's wonderful, Nate."

I said, "And I'm moving. I'm moving across town. But I can still come here for the band."

She said, "You lost me, Nate. Where are you moving to?"

I took a breath and tried to slow down. I said, "I'm moving across town close to Bunting Public. But I want to be able to come here. You know, because Bunting doesn't have a band. And I really love the flute." I let out another breath.

She said, "Oh, yes. There's another student, Charlotte. She came here from across town for our great music studies."

I said, "Yeah, I know. I need to do that, too."

"Well, I'll have to talk to your music teacher about it, Nate. But I'm sure if you really want to be in the band, we can work it out."

I said, "Okay, thanks, Mrs. Berger. I have to go now." I turned and walked out of the office. The office gave me the creeps. Also, I wanted to leave before she changed her mind. I let out a "phew." I was so happy. The flute was turning out to be a real lifesaver.

phew!

November 20

Today was my first band practice. Miss Mirel tapped her stick on her music stand. Everyone looked at her.

Then she said, "Everyone, we have a new member in the band. Nate Brown." She held her arm in my direction.

I was sitting in the front row. I turned around a little and looked back. There were about twenty kids staring at me. I looked at the flute girls sitting beside me. I gave a half smile. Then I sat a little lower in my seat.

"Nate is the first boy flutist we have ever had in the school band," Miss Mirel said.

I put my hand up to my face and sunk even lower in my seat. Trevor and Jason would have laughed really loudly at that. The first boy flutist. Just put a sign on me that says "geek." Even the girls in my music class would have laughed.

But no one in the band laughed. It figures. I guess they think being the first boy flutist is cool. They're so weird.

I know a couple of the kids from my music class. Some are from the other grade eight music classes. And some are grade seven kids. Almost all the girls who play flute are in grade seven.

Miss Mirel tapped her stick again and we all started playing. The kids in the band are way better than my music class. When they play, all the instruments sound good together. It actually sounds like a song. That's not what my music class sounds like at all.

Miss Mirel had to stop the class a couple of times to show me the right beat. I felt like a geek. I'll have to take my flute home and practice if I'm going to pull this off.

November 21 @

4 p.m. — The living room

Frankie came up to me in the hall this morning.

He said, "Hey Nate, how was band practice last night? How's everyone's favorite flute player?" He hit me in the arm.

I said, "Very funny. It's the only way I can stay at Emery. I'm only doing it because I have to."

He said, "Yeah, yeah, yeah. So who else is in the band?"

I said, "No one."

Frankie said, "Are you the only guy with a flute again?"

I said, "Yeah. It gets better. I'm the only guy *ever* to play flute in the band." Frankie laughed a little. So I said, "Shut up."

He asked me who else plays flute. So I told him it was just a bunch of grade seven girls. Frankie says that's a gold mine. I should pay attention to them. He says those are the girls I'll want to date in high school. He says Monty dates younger girls all the time.

8 p.m. — My bedroom

My parents announced today that they have bought our new house. They asked Tammy and me at dinner if we wanted to drive by it. What's the point? I don't care what the outside of the new house looks like. All the houses on the other side of town look like crap. All I know is I have to play flute in the stupid school band. I don't want to see the new house until I have to.

I said, "No thanks."

My mom said, "Really? I think you'll like it. It's just over on—"

"Yeah, I know where it is," I said. "I don't want to go there."

She said, "All right, fine. What about you, Tammy? Do you want to drive by?"

Tammy looked at me, then back at my mom. She crossed her arms and frowned. She was not happy about having to go to a new school. "No. I don't want to see the new house. I'm staying here with Nate."

My mom said, "Okay, you two. I don't understand why not. But suit yourselves."

From: "Mistacruz"
To: "NateB"
Subject: Skate or die!

Martin Cruz, the skater guy, just e-mailed me. I forgot that we had given each other our e-mail addresses. He sent me a link for another skater web site. It's cool. It's by this older guy in high school. He's really good. He even has a sponsor. A company gives him free skateboarding clothes. All he has to do is wear the clothes in the competitions. You have to be really good for that.

Martin is going to be at Skate Max after Christmas. It's this competition in an indoor skatepark across town. I can hardly wait.

I should ask him if he knows about that skater girl. The one with the orange and pink hat with the pom-pom.

November 24 🌀

Today at school something weird happened to my locker. I saw Frankie down the hall and asked him what was going on.

He said, "Suki and Ashley decorated our locker."

I said, "Yeah, I can see that." Silver paper and red bows. Great. There was also a huge bell tied to the lock.

Frankie said, "It's for the locker-decorating competition."

I said, "Why can't they just decorate their own dumb locker?"

He said, "They did. They did ours, too."

I said, "Why?"

Frankie said, "I told Suki they could."

I said, "Why?"

Frankie said, "Because she's my girlfriend."

AH! Oh well, she's his girlfriend. That settles it, then. Of course. Right. She can do anything she wants. She's his girlfriend. Who can argue with that? Whatever!

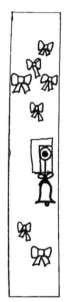

November 25 ≋

I can't believe this. Being in the band just gets worse and worse.

We have to play in front of the school at the holiday assembly. I just found out at today's band practice. Why did I take Miranda's advice? She's not even in the band. She doesn't have to suffer through it.

It's times like this that I think changing schools would be easier. So I'd have no friends. At least I wouldn't have to deal with the flute.

I wonder if Miss Mirel will let me sit in the back row.

November 27 ≪

The living room — One end of the sofa

My grandma and grandpa are here. They flew all the way from the coast. We hardly ever see them. My Aunt Camille and Uncle Roger are also here. They brought my cousins, Mike and Lisa. They are around the same ages as me and Tammy. When we were younger they used to break all our toys. We hid our stuff if we knew they were coming.

Mike is a year younger than me. He's in the band at his school. My mom told him I'm in the band at my school, too. Now he wants to follow me around all day. He asked me if we can practice our instruments. As if! He actually brought his with him. It's a French horn. First of all, I didn't bring my flute home for the weekend. Second of all, the flute and the French horn? How weird would that sound together?

My dad, my uncle, and my grandpa are watching football. I don't watch football much, but I think I could get into it. My grandma is sitting at

the end of the sofa. She's sewing something. She just asked why the players keep on stopping. And why they won't just let each other run for a while. Clearly she does not get it.

Before dinner Aunt Camille asked what I wanted for Christmas. I said a cell phone. My mom and dad looked at each other and laughed. That means one of two things. One: they have already bought me a cell phone. Or two: they will never in a million years buy me a cell phone.

My Uncle Roger asked me what I think about the new house. I told him I haven't seen it yet.

He laughed and said, "Yes you have. You see it every day."

I said, "No, I haven't. My parents wanted to take me to see it, but I didn't want to go."

"Take you to see it? Ha!" he said loudly. Just then my dad walked into the dining room. He was carrying the turkey.

He said, "Okay everybody, here it is!"

I think my Uncle Roger is losing it.

December 5

3:30 p.m. — The bus, back seat

My whole class is on a school bus. We're on our way back from the skating rink. The grade eights go on a skating trip every year. Trevor and Jason found old hockey sticks in the penalty box. They were skating around and pretending to take slap shots. Then Mr. Sweet took the sticks away.

I like skating. But there's not much to do. Besides go around and around and around. At least I'm not one of those kids who hold on to the boards. Or one of the kids who just stand in the middle. Or fall on their butt if anyone comes near them.

I looked around for Miranda. She was skating with some girls from another class. A group of kids were watching something at the other end of the rink. The guys and I skated over to see.

Everyone had formed a big circle. They were watching Ashley. She skated backward and then turned forward. All of a sudden she was doing a spin. She put her leg out behind her. She leaned back and raised her arms above her head. It was pretty cool, actually. Then she stopped spinning.

"Cool!" said someone behind me.

"Do something else," said another kid.

"Yeah, do a triple toe loop!" Trevor shouted.

"I can't do a triple toe loop," Ashley said. The circle of kids started to break up.

I skated over to her. I said, "I never knew you were a figure skater."

She said, "Yeah." And then Russ VanHolt skated over to us.

"Do you want to skate around?" he said to her.

She said, "Yeah, sure. I'd love to." She looked at me and simply said, "Bye, Nate." And they skated off together.

Oh, so I guess she's all into Russ VanHolt now. That's fine. In fact I couldn't be happier. I don't know what she thinks is so great about him, though. One time he showed up at Ramesh's to try tricks on his ramp. He could barely even do an ollie. He was too scared to do a 180 off the ramp. Whatever. I'm just glad she's not hanging around me all the time. Very glad. Very very glad.

ramp

December 13 ☼

There are only twelve days until Christmas. I did all my Christmas shopping today. I wasn't going to go shopping. But Jason called me and said we should go to the mall. He had to get Christmas presents, too. He has it even worse than me—three sisters!

We looked around for a long time. First we looked in the video store. We checked all the new games. I saw a few DVD box sets I liked. Then we looked in the pet store. Jason showed me the type of snake his brother bought. Next we went to the CD store and then to the store that only has knives. I couldn't find anything for my mom, or Tammy, or my dad.

"I can't go home without presents," Jason said.

I said, "I know. This sucks. I have no idea what to get."

Jason asked, "What do girls like?"

I said, "I don't know. Maybe we should watch girls and see what they look at." It was the best idea I'd had in a long time. I couldn't believe I hadn't thought of it before. All we had to do was follow some girls and watch what they bought.

We saw three girls walking toward the department store. We followed them in but stayed far behind them. We didn't want them to think we were following them. They went straight to the perfumes. Jason and I stood behind a rack of sweaters. We pretended to look at them.

The girls were all talking at once. They were picking up all the bottles and smelling them.

"Can I help you, gentlemen?"

"Huh?" I said. A lady with a gold nametag was standing beside us.

"Are you looking for a sweater for your mother?" she asked.

I said, "Oh, uh, yeah. Thanks. We're just going to keep looking."

She said, "Okay." She walked away and then looked back a couple of times. Jason and I pretended to look at sweaters. Just then the girls walked away from the perfumes.

I said, "Jason, did you see what ones they sprayed on themselves?"

Jason said, "Yeah, it was that tall, blue bottle." We waited until the girls were out of sight. Then we walked over to the perfumes. Jason picked up the tall, blue bottle from all the other bottles. He smelled it. Another woman with light blond hair walked up to us.

She said, "Do you like that one?"

Jason said, "Yeah, I guess."

The woman said, "Is it a gift?"

Jason said, "Maybe. How much is it?"

"Sixty dollars," she said.

Jason said, "Oh!" We both looked down at the blue bottles. "How much for the smaller bottle?"

She said, "I was talking about the smaller bottle." Jason put the bottle down. The woman said, "I can show you something else that's nice." She showed us some other bottles. "These are sprays that all the girls are wearing. They're nice and they are very well priced."

Jason bought three bottles for his three sisters. I bought one bottle for my sister.

Next stop was the men's department. Both dads are getting a blue tie and two pairs of socks—one brown, one black. Then we went up to the second level. That's where all the glasses and bed sheets are. There was a big table full of tall red candles. We bought two. One for Jason's mom. One for mine. Christmas shopping: complete.

December 14

Today my mom asked me what I want for Christmas. I said that I wanted not to move. She said that it was hardly moving. I don't know what she means. Hardly moving? How is moving hardly moving? Either you're moving or you're not. And we are. Moving is SO moving.

She said that I will love the new house.

I said, "No I won't."

She asked why I said that. I told her that she and Dad are messing up my life. She said I was being silly. How can she say that? I think making your kids change schools is a pretty big deal.

She said we could still drive past the new house if I wanted. Then I could see that it's really nice. She says my room is bigger. And there's a pool with a slide. Usually I would think that was cool. But I won't be happy going down a slide with no friends. I told her that. She said my friends could come over anytime. She's missing the point.

Anyway, I told her I don't want to drive by the house. I don't want to see it. I don't even want to think about it. Then I said I had to go practice the flute. I said that was all her fault, too. She just looked at me.

Then she said, "Okay, and while you're up there, clean up your room. It's getting kind of messy again."

December 19 ◎

Boys' bathroom — second stall from the right

I don't think I will ever live this down. The whole school is in the gym. I am in the bathroom. With my stupid flute, I might add. I have to go on stage with the band in less than five minutes. Miss Mirel just told me one of the flute girls is sick. So I have to take her spot. I am going to have to play part of a song by myself. Great. I told Miss Mirel it should be one of the other girls. I told her I'm not very good. She said that I have become one of the best flute players. She said I have to do it.

I can't believe this. I can't believe I have become good at flute. I can't believe that I have to play all by myself in front of the whole school. What if I screw up? Playing the flute all by yourself is bad enough. Screwing up a song in front of the school AND my family would just be brutal.

To make matters worse, I'm wearing a Santa hat. A Santa hat! It was either that or a red Rudolph  nose. One of the flute girls took the last Santa hat. I begged her for the hat. Finally I had to trade her my locker mirror for the hat. Well actually, Suki's locker mirror. Ha.

9:45 p.m. — My bedroom

I am so glad that is over. It's now my number one worst moment ever. Number two is getting pantsed on the first day of school. Number three was when I farted last year during a spelling test.

First we had to march in a single file into the gym. It was a full house. The whole gym was set up with chairs. We had to walk right down the middle.

Jason, Trevor, Frankie, and Ramesh were sitting together. Jason yelled "Yeah, Nate!" when I walked by.

Playing the flute in band is bad enough. But a whole gym full of people watching me really sucks. What's worse is that they all think that I play the flute because I like it. They don't know that I'm only doing this because I have to. They don't know I'm faking it. I wanted to tell them all that this is just a means to an end. It's not like it seems. This is not me. I am not Nate, the flute lover.

We took our places in the chairs set up at the front of the gym. We started playing "Jingle Bells." My part was coming up in the third song. The first song ended. Everyone clapped.

The second song started. "Frosty the Snowman." I wanted it to last forever. It ended. More clapping.

Then came the third song, "Silver Bells." Miss Mirel tapped her stick on her stand. She looked at me and winked. I felt myself start to throw up. I gulped and tried not to puke.

We started playing. I kept my eyes on the music book. It just looked like a bunch of lines and dots. I couldn't remember what the notes were. Keeping my flute up at my mouth, I looked to my side. All the flute girls were blowing perfectly into their flutes. They rocked back and forth a little bit as they played.

I looked back at my music book. I knew where we were on the sheet. I just couldn't read the notes. I learned how to read them in music class. But my heart was pounding. They just looked like lines with dots at the bottom. I couldn't remember which line was which. I couldn't even remember "Every Good Boy Deserves Fudge." My part was coming up on the next page. The song reached the end of the music on that page. Everyone reached down and flipped their pages over. I took a deep breath. It was all over.

To my surprise I could read the music. Someone had written the notes in pencil under the lines. I played.

Then my part was over. I played the rest of the song with the others. Then I sank back in my chair and set my flute on my lap.

When the band was finished we all stood up to take a bow. The parents and students started clapping. But I noticed a few people in the front row pointing at me. I looked farther back into the sea of faces. Jason, Trevor, Ramesh, and Frankie were laughing their heads off. Ramesh pointed down. I looked down. The water that forms inside the flute had spilled out. There was flute spit all over my pants. I heard a click and a big flash went

off. I shut my eyes tight. I opened them again. Suki was just lowering her camera. Great! That's one for the yearbook!

December 24 ☺

The night before Christmas — My bedroom

Tonight we went over to my parents' friends' house. I drank a lot of eggnog. It was the first time I have ever had it. I always thought it sounded gross. A drink made of eggs? No thanks. But tonight, my dad's friend Jerry made me drink eggnog. It was good. I couldn't believe it.

December 25 3.?

9 a.m. — The living room

It's Christmas. I woke up at seven a.m. I went downstairs. Tammy was already there sitting quietly beside the tree. I say "tree," but really it's just a giant plant. My parents put lights on it. We have to move on New Year's Day. So they packed all the decorations. Tammy put a silver star on top that she made in art. But it's not really the same as a real tree.

We waited a full hour for my parents to wake up. I started a pot of coffee. I thought the smell of it might wake them up. I watched Trevor make coffee at his house that one time. But I couldn't really remember how many scoops to put in. I just guessed. Ten seemed like a good number. While we waited, we staked out all the presents. Finally Mom and Dad woke up and came downstairs.

It took exactly 28 minutes to open the presents.

My dad took a sip of his coffee and said, "WOW! Merry Christmas!" He looked at my mom. She smelled her coffee, and they smiled at each other.

I said, "What? Did I do it right?"

My dad said, "It's fine, Nate. Thanks for making it."

I got some good stuff. A CD stereo. A new computer game. A year's worth of Skateboarding magazines. Cool. Oh, and the usual filler stuff. You know, socks, underwear, T-shirts, boots, pants, shirts, sweaters. I refuse to go back-to-school shopping. So my mom makes up for it. She always gives me new clothes for Christmas. No cell phone though. I didn't really expect to get one. But you can't blame a guy for trying.

Tammy liked the spray I got her. And my parents liked their stuff, too. Now the whole living room is a

85

sea of wrapping paper. My parents have gone upstairs to get dressed. Tammy is reading the backs of her new books.

My parents have also packed all the pots and pans in boxes. We're having Chinese take-out for Christmas dinner. I'm pretty happy about that.

December 31 ꣑⁝

5 p.m. — New Year's Eve

Some New Year's Eve. Our entire house is in boxes. We can hardly even move. Even my bed is packed up. All I have is a mattress on the floor and my sleeping bag.

My parents are going out for dinner. Tammy is babysitting for our neighbors. What am I doing? Nothing. Of course there's nothing good going on. Well I guess I'll just watch TV by myself. That's just great. I'm thirteen years old, and I'm not going out on New Year's Eve. I might as well be babysitting with Tammy.

5:05 p.m.

Just great. I turned on the TV, and my
parents have shut off the cable. I can just barely
make out about three shows.

8 p.m. — My bedroom

Ramesh just called. His parents said he could invite
people over. I called my dad and mom on their cell
phone. They said I could walk over there. But I have
to come straight home after midnight. I told them
that midnight is just when the party gets started.

My mom just said, "Nate, straight home."
Hello. I'm thirteen, people.

At least I'm not sitting at home by myself.
Watching a dumb New Year's special on TV. Or
wishing I was watching a dumb New Year's special
because we have no cable.

12:30 a.m.

I'm never listening to my parents again. Here I am at home, and they aren't even home yet. I could have stayed longer at Ramesh's party.

And I was right. Things were just getting started. AND it was a high school party. Ramesh's older sister and brother had friends over. There was no stupid Spin the Bottle at this party. I was hoping that Miranda would be there. Ramesh said he called some girls. But none could come because it was such late notice. So it was just me, Ramesh, Trevor, Jason, and Frankie.

Ramesh's sister is in grade nine. So I guess it's just as well that none of the grade eight girls were there. The grade nine girls were talking to us the whole time. One of them kissed Ramesh at midnight!

Then everyone sat around listening to music and laughing. Except for me. I had to come straight home!

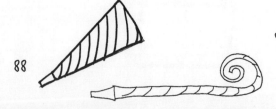

Jan 1

Moving day — My mattress

Almost everything is in the moving van. It's only nine a.m. I can hear the moving men on their way upstairs. I didn't think moving men even worked on New Year's Day. I guess these ones do. The only thing left up in my room is this mattress. I guess this is it.

9:15 a.m. — My new house

The men put my mattress in the truck. Then they closed the back door and shut the lock. The truck drove out of the driveway and up the street. My mom walked through the house to make sure we hadn't forgot anything. We piled in the car and left for our new house across town.

We pulled out of the driveway and drove up the street. I thought to myself that this would be the last time that I would drive up this street. I looked out the back window. My old house got farther and farther away. My throat felt dry. I turned around. Tammy was sitting quietly. Her arms were folded across her chest. She had a huge frown on her face.

My dad turned left onto the main road. We drove for a block and then he turned left onto the next street.

I said, "Where are we going?"

My mom said, "To our new house."

I said, "But why are we going this—" I stopped talking. A moving truck was parked down the street. It looked just like the one that had been at our house. We got closer. There were the moving men that had just been at our house. They were unlocking the back door of the truck. I said, "Why are they stopping here?"

My dad laughed a little. "Because this is our new house. Jeez, Nate."

"What? *This* is our new house!" I yelled.

"Holy freak out," said Tammy.

I said, "What about the house on Rideout?"

My mom said, "We never said we bought that house. We only looked at it. This house was better, so we bought it instead."

"But—" I said.

"This is a great house, Nate. And close to your friends. You won't even have to change schools. Aren't you happy?" my mom said.

"But I joined the band," was all I could say. No one tells me anything.

My dad said, "And now you don't have to quit." He pulled up behind the moving truck. The movers lifted my mattress down the ramp. "Okay, everyone out. Let's move!"

So here I am. In my new bedroom. I'm looking out the window. I can see my old house from here. So much for good-bye. I can't say I'm upset. I couldn't be happier. Moving isn't so bad. And this place has a pool. With a slide! The best news is that my days in the school band are over.

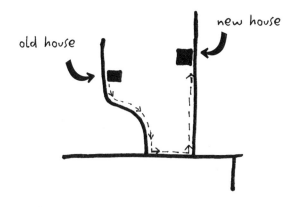

Glossary

180
A half turn done in the air on a skateboard, from a ramp

assembly
A group of people gathered for a common purpose

competition
A contest

eggnog
A drink that is made with eggs and milk

equation
A math formula

Every Good Boy Deserves Fudge
A sentence to help remember EGBDF, which are notes on a music scale

hoops
A slang term for a practice game of basketball

ollie
A trick in which one hops in the air while on
a skateboard

pantsed
To have one's pants pulled down in public

prank
A practical joke

real estate agent
A person who helps others sell and buy a house

slap shot
Hitting a puck with a hockey stick in one fast
motion

sponsor
A person or company who pays for equipment in
return for advertising

symphony
A long concert of classical music

Other books by K.E. Calder and Tea Leaf Press

Spend the summer with Mel Randall and Will Bergeron! The novels in the **Deer Lake** series follow the summer cottage adventures of two young teens and their group of friends.

Summer of Change by H.J. Lewis

Every year, Mel Randall can't wait to spend the summer at Deer Lake. But not this summer. Mel's best friend has moved away. The general store has new owners. Everything is changing. Then Mel has an adventure and meets Ian Suwan. Maybe a little change isn't so bad after all.

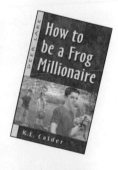

How to be a Frog Millionaire by K.E. Calder

Will Bergeron is stuck at his grandma's cottage for the whole summer. To make matters worse, his bratty twin cousins are there, too. Will is the only guy his age without a summer job. He comes up with a plan to make money. Will just has to hope his grandma doesn't find out.
ISBN 1-55068-126-5

Who is Mel Randall, Anyway? by H.J. Lewis

Mel Randall's new neighbor, Diana, is nothing like Mel. Diana cares more about clothes, nail polish, and magazines. She gives Mel a makeover. Mel's friend, Allison, likes the old Mel. Diana's cute brother, Ted, likes the new Mel. The question is: who is the real Mel Randall?
ISBN 1-55068-128-1

The Stalker by K.E. Calder

A dark figure on a stormy night. A set of lost keys. A body bag. No one knows how old Beatrice Jones disappeared from Deer Lake. All the clues point to Booker. He's the grumpy old man in the cottage next door. Can Will prove that Booker is a murderer? Or will he become Booker's next victim?
ISBN 1-55068-124-9

Stranded by K.E. Calder

The worst has happened. Will is trapped at a cottage with Mel Randall and her two sisters. How will he survive for two whole weeks? Living in a house full of girls is more than Will expected. He has a secret to keep from Mel. Will he tell her when they become lost on a dark, foggy night?
ISBN 1-55068-122-2

The Secret of the Bailey Bay Inn by K.E. Calder

Weird things are happening at the Bailey Bay Inn. The old hotel is boarded up. It has been deserted for years. Or has it? Will does some research on the run-down building. He learns the truth about its terrible past. Now are Will and his friends in danger?
ISBN 1-55068-097-8

The Accidental Camper by H.J. Lewis

A canoe trip, a cool counselor, and her best friends. Life can't get much better than this for Mel Randall. Except for a few small details. Mel fights with her boyfriend. Her two friends hate each other. And Diana doesn't know one end of a canoe paddle from the other. This trip is turning out to be more than Mel bargained for!
ISBN 1-55068-119-2

For more information, visit www.tealeafpress.com

Special Thanks

Billy Bleich, Alexander DeBoo, Nathan Bennet